P9-DBY-183

My Summer Vacation

A Random House PICTUREBACK®

My Summer Vacation

By Sumiko

Random House 🏠 **New York**

First American Edition, 1990. Copyright © 1987, 1990 by Sumiko Davies. All rights reserved under International and Pan-American Copyright Conventions. Published in the United States by Random House, Inc., New York. Originally published in Great Britain as *My Holiday* by William Heinemann Ltd., London, in 1987.

Library of Congress Cataloging-in-Publication Data:
Sumiko. My summer vacation. (A Random House pictureback) British ed. has title: My holiday. SUMMARY: A little girl describes the many things she and her family do on their camping vacation. [1. Camping–Fiction. 2. Vacation–Fiction. 3. Family life–Fiction] I. Title. II. Series. PZ7.S9539My 1990 [E] 89-43164 ISBN 0-679-80525-7 ISBN 0-679-90525-1 (lib. bdg.)

Manufactured in the United States of America   1 2 3 4 5 6 7 8 9 10

Today we are going on a vacation. Here I am with
my brother Ned. We have our backpacks! We are
both ready to go.

Mom and Dad are busy packing the trailer. There
are so many things we have to take. We don't want
to forget anything!

Our trailer is like a small house on wheels.
It has everything we need—a stove, a refrigerator,
even a toilet.

I like to pretend it is my house and my doll Tina is my little girl.

Dad hitches the trailer to the car and we are
on our way. Ned takes a nap, but not me!
I play "I Spy" with Mom.

We stop at a park to have a picnic. I eat not one but two sandwiches. "The fresh air is giving us all big appetites," says Dad.

At last we reach the campground. Ned and I put
on our swimsuits and run down to the beach.

"Race you to the water, Ned!" I shout. We can't
wait to get wet.

Our campsite is in the woods. Mom and Dad put
up the tent for us to sleep in. I help too.

There are other families at the campground. I wonder if I will find someone to play with.

That night Dad cooks hamburgers in the trailer.
We eat on the folding table. I like having dinner
outside.

It's fun going to bed in our tent. Ned and I have
sleeping bags right next to each other. Mom tucks
us in, just like at home.

The next day we go swimming. *Wheee!* Dad
swings me around in the waves. I love how it feels!

I make friends with Michelle. "Let's draw pictures in the sand," I say. We draw a great big face!

Michelle shows me her secret pool between the rocks. Ooooh, the water is so warm. Ned catches tiny crabs nearby.

Later we collect things on the beach. Ned finds
some seaweed. Michelle and I look for pretty
shells. What a nice collection we have!

One day we go on a walk. The trail up the hill is
steep. "Wait for me!" says Ned. But I can't wait.
Mom says I run like a rabbit.

At the top of the hill there is a meadow. I help Ned catch butterflies. After we catch them, we let them go.

Another day I go exploring with my new friends.
"Look! I caught a toad!" cries Michelle's brother.
Suddenly it starts to rain.

We run into the trailer, where it is cozy and dry.
We play games until it stops raining.

The next day we rent a boat and sail out to an island. What a day! The wind blows our boat across the water.

On the island Mom and Dad go snorkeling. I play
in a rubber raft with Ned. I can see under the
water with a mask.

The water is warm and clear. There are lots of fish swimming below.

I shout, "Look, Ned! There's a whole other world right under our raft."

Tonight we are having a cookout. Dad makes a fire
and cooks chicken and hot dogs over the hot coals.

Dad lets me cook my own hot dog. We need a
lantern to help us see. It's fun to be outdoors when
it's dark.

After dinner Dad lights some sparklers. He lets me hold one, but I have to be very careful. Wow! They are so exciting to watch.

Just before we go to bed Mom tells us stories about the night sky. The stars are so bright!

Our summer vacation is over. We pack everything in the trailer and head home. Good-bye! See you next year!